Mingyuan Hu

Late Roses and Early Snow

Hermits United
London · Paris

Published in Great Britain by Hermits United Ltd. 2022

Copyright © Mingyuan Hu 2022
The moral rights of the author have been asserted

Typeset by Fabrizio Cosenza
Printed in France

A catalogue record for this book is available from the British Library
ISBN 978-1-9998833-2-4

www.hermits-united.com

Late Roses and Early Snow

One

1

Three days after Mark's arrival at Giacomo's palazzo, Italy went into lockdown. From his window Mark contemplated Brunelleschi's dome against the sky's silence. Since the dome's existence, Florence had seen a few plagues. Quarantines were practised, as were lockdowns. In history, variations upon a theme recur, albeit at long intervals. Human memories are not generally long enough to hear history's refrains.

Mark was attentive to this music. He was a historian. Renaissance humanists' rapport with the past was one with which he was at ease. But that is not why we find him in Florence this early spring, contemplating Brunelleschi's dome against the sky's silence.

Giacomo had invited Mark to stay a month with him to decipher some archival material. Documents from a provincial archive in China were being thrown out a few years ago when, with an artist's help, Giacomo purchased a fraction of them. Lorenzo, Giacomo's son who taught French Literature at Oxford, suggested that a colleague specialising in Chinese and European History visit his father and take a look.

2

Mark was on sabbatical when Lorenzo rang. He knew not what the documents were about, nor why Giacomo had collected them. Without much deliberation, he flew in from London.

Behind a bronze door near Piazza San Firenze was a hermit's den. Giacomo lived alone. Mark was greeted by the reserved old man and shown directly to his work space: two enormous rooms, one filled with documents, the other housing a single antique desk. Inherited from Giacomo's quattrocento forebears, the palazzo overlooked a stately courtyard. The top floor was at Mark's disposal.

So it was that three days later Mark and Giacomo sat face to face in the grand salon with five metres' distance between them.

'You are most welcome to stay for the lockdown,' said Giacomo.

Mark thanked him. 'I quickly went through the documents; they are varied in kind. I'm now looking at persecution files of the so-called rightists in the city of Wuhan from the late fifties.'

Giacomo looked gloomily down. Only some weeks ago, the name of Wuhan would not have jarred.

3

Sitting in the Rococo room with a dusty archive transported from Maoist China, Mark felt physically ill. He had come upon a dossier of a young man, a student of Literature at the University of Wuhan, who in September 1957 was condemned in the Anti-Rightist Campaign. He was twenty-one.

There was nothing special about the case. Millions were arbitrarily condemned. Many committed suicide. All suffered the insufferable. Mark had known about this. Over and over he read the forced self-criticism (that every literate person, every intellectual had to produce) of this young man written in 1957, then twice more in 1959. Page after page, the culprit laid bare his incorrect thoughts and concluded that they were wrong. 'I was opposed to the slogan "Ample, Fast, Good, Thrifty" (the national goal in economic production) being applied to research in the humanities. I was wrong. I thought that research could not be good if it were fast, ample and thrifty. I was wrong. I was wrong because I was a rightist.'

Mark thought this a grotesque testimony to the mass process of brainwashing. Then he read it again. And again. He became unsure if it wasn't a desperate act of resistance. The condemned said he was wrong – there was no alternative – *but elucidated all the same that which was supposed to be wrong.* In other words, he *still thought* that research could not be good if it were fast, ample and thrifty, all the while saying he was wrong to think so.

4

Giacomo's settecento forebears must have loved chinoiserie. Decoration in the house, other than late Renaissance and Baroque frescos, was sparse, consisting mainly of exquisite Ming porcelain.

Giacomo grew up amidst the finest things and read the finest literature. As a child he devoured Homer and Li Tai-po. Equally accomplished at the cello and at the easel, at seventeen he stood six foot four, a quadrilingual cosmopolite. Law was his chosen profession, and family wealth ensured discreet and extravagant means to pursue his intellectual interests. Once, Giacomo financed two political scientists' in-depth research on the Vichy regime; later, he commissioned a historical project that chronicled Italy's dealings in Africa under Mussolini. Interactions with researchers were intense, while Giacomo stayed publicly anonymous. In the early eighties, two composers and a writer received his patronage after defecting from East Berlin, without ever learning of the philanthropist's identity.

In 1973 Giacomo was twenty-six and passing through Venice. There he chanced upon Michelangelo Antonioni's documentary on contemporary China. What he saw resembled nothing of the poetry he had read in his childhood of that great civilisation.

Even as an adolescent, Giacomo was indifferent to the communist movements everywhere fervent in his youth. He guarded against political passion of a fanatical kind, left and right alike. In 1973, passing through Venice, Giacomo had not only to reconcile the ancient land of the most refined poetry with what appeared to be an ideological laboratory, but to try and fathom the human dignity on the pre-consumerist faces in Antonioni's film. The China he saw defied his political notions. Condemnation seemed flippant. Judgement seemed trivial. What he needed, thought Giacomo, was more than exact knowledge. What was called for was imagination.

5

Giacomo found Mark sitting motionless in the courtyard by the fountain. Quietly sitting down on the opposite side, he greeted him with a smile.

Mark smiled back. 'How are you, sir?'

'Quite well. Yourself?'

'Lightly puzzled.'

'How so?'

'Two things. I wonder what to do with the files. I wonder what you might wish that we do with them.'

'It is your decision. It is your material. As for me, I would like to understand what happened – what happened to the individuals – through your understanding.'

'That's a remarkable disposition, sir. Perhaps as much as this material, your intellectual curiosity astounds me. After spending two weeks with the archive, I'm concerned precisely with the individuals. One in particular preoccupies my thoughts.'

'Do tell.'

'A student got himself into trouble because he openly said that universities should be administered by academics and not by the Party. He was labelled a rightist in 1957, forced to self-criticise, was reeducated twice in camps in 1958, and was still writing self-criticism in 1959. Being little interested in meta-narratives, I am not tempted, for instance, to study the Anti-Rightist Campaign using files in this archive. What I want to know is what happened to the troubled not only during but *after* the campaign. What became of this young man, as a matter of fact? What did the collective experience of absurdity, of injustice done to one, amount to when endured by a single human being? And when this being later lived, *if* he lived, in times less absurd and less unjust, what were the lingering implications, if any, for him and for those close to him? Could he trust? Could he love?'

Affected by Mark's sudden but composed articulation, Giacomo nodded inwardly. When he asked Lorenzo for the recommendation of a scholar who read Chinese, Lorenzo said that Mark was one with the rare gift of imagination.

'I share your enquiry,' said Giacomo. 'Would you like to go to China and find out?'

Fixing his gaze pensively at the fountain, Mark paused for a long while before responding in a low voice: 'I think I may already know.'

6

Mark first saw Rosanna in the Bodleian Library twenty-one years ago. Behind a pile of books, her face bore a concentration that verged on gravity. One week later, both present at a friend's party, they talked to each other until after midnight, and met up the next morning to continue the conversation. They had been inseparable since.

Mark never knew anyone vaguely resembling Rosanna. By all appearances, Rosanna did not resemble her own parents. Her English mother went to Beijing in 1978 to study at the Central Academy of Fine Arts. There she fell in love with Rosanna's father, a poet. They were soon married, and Rosanna was born a year later.

When Rosanna was ten, her mother left China definitively, taking Rosanna with her, her career as a painter to develop back in England. Rosanna was raised by her maternal grandparents in Hampstead until she went to Oxford to read History.

Once a year Rosanna would receive a letter from her father from Beijing. Twice or thrice a year her mother would call. Neither her parents expressed any wish to see her. The Rosanna that Mark met in 1999 seemed to him both a child and an old soul. His love for her meant, amongst other things, to fathom the unfathomable. Rosanna bore her parents no reproach. She would speak of them, tears in her eyes, with sorrow and compassion, and Mark would look in amazement at a fierce intellectual without cynicism, an abandoned child without bitterness or blame.

He did all the blaming for her, in all the years after her death.

7

Sitting motionless by the fountain, Mark pondered for the thousandth time the last entry in Rosanna's journal. '17th November 2004. To live has meant for me: to surmount life. I pray to God that there be enough force in me to bring life to another being.'

Rosanna died giving birth on 30 November 2004, in Oxford. Their son Luke lived for a few hours, dying in Mark's arms. Mark had since inhabited a winter that never ended. Each evening, the twenty-nine-year-old newly appointed Lecturer in Renaissance Studies would return home from his office, turn on the light, and sit for hours in Rosanna's study.

For many years, he kept Rosanna's study exactly as it was. For many years, he could not forgive himself for having wanted, more than Rosanna had, to have a child.

He could not forgive Rosanna's father for having sent Rosanna a letter that made her last days inconsolable.

8

Seeing Mark's gaunt figure in his courtyard, Giacomo decided that they ought henceforth to dine together. Since his arrival, Mark had insisted on running his own errands and preparing his own meals. But to Giacomo he looked either insufficiently rested or insufficiently fed.

Most of Europe had by then followed Italy's suit in locking down. On top of a vicious virus, aggravated precarity beset the less privileged. Since the beginning of the pandemic, Giacomo had sought to send aid to regions most affected by the disease.

Giacomo's own solitary routine had little changed. A butler and a cook had worked for him for thirty-odd years. The tranquillity of the palazzo was however not without tumult. Two days earlier, the butler learned that his sister had been admitted to intensive care in Turin after contracting Covid. He was distressed, and had a chat with Mark and Giacomo after dinner, before excusing himself.

In his gentle intonation, Giacomo said: 'I enjoyed our conversation about the archive, Mark. Thank you. Lorenzo told me that your mastery of Chinese is phenomenal. That you could interpret any text, ancient or modern, with ease. And that despite this total command of the written language, you do not speak a word of it.'

'I learned Chinese', Mark replied, 'when I was thirty, to be able to read my wife's notes.'

'Is she a historian of China?'

'No. She was a Renaissance scholar, like me.' After a pause, Mark added: 'She lived her childhood in Beijing.'

'I see.' Sensing Mark's reticence, Giacomo asked: 'I hope your family in England are doing well?'

'They are, and thank you, sir, for asking. I spoke to my parents on the phone yesterday. I'm grateful that they never divorced. Now they look after each other.'

'I understand.' And after a pause, Giacomo said: 'Lorenzo's mother and I are not divorced either. Though we haven't seen each other in years. And we do not look after each other.'

'How come? – if you do not mind my asking, sir.'

'Oh, long story. She is the exact opposite of me. I think I married her to defy myself,' Giacomo said wryly, to Mark's smile. 'We met in Paris – she is French, and I was there on a self-motivated trip of sociological research – in 1968, in the heat of the student movement. Politically, we disagreed on everything. She was an ardent participant, and I a dispassionate bystander. But our difference did not frighten me – I saw it as an existential investigation. You see... my entire marriage was based on a hypothesis, that love is unconditional.'

'Which means?'

'Which means: love transcends difference; love pardons the unpardonable.'

'And what might be the result of your investigation?'

'That love transcends difference. That love pardons the unpardonable. It was by all means a happy union. Until one day I came home to find Inès in bed with another man. She didn't want a divorce. Lorenzo was only eight. So I let her choose how she would like to live. She wanted to take Lorenzo with her and go back to Paris, so I supported it. It has been thirty years and she still does not want a divorce, so I never demand it.'

'All this to prove your hypothesis valid?'

'All this to not betray the hypothesis even when I have been betrayed.'

'And you do not consider yourself in the least idealistic?' Marvelled Mark, his eyes now wide open.

9

Giacomo did not consider himself idealistic. The word 'idealism' had been so tinted by ideals of all colours that he shunned it.

Just as a single idea reigned over his marriage, Giacomo's entire life was governed by an almost antique force: his love for virtue.

Lovers of virtue do not necessarily consider themselves virtuous. Simply, their hearts obey a higher order, in secret.

Lovers of virtue are not necessarily virtuous. Some heed the order through their acts. Some don't.

10

Though his lifeforce may be antique, Giacomo's idea of love came of a Romantic stock.

For the ancient Greeks, love meant admiration. Giacomo adored but did not admire Inès.

Did he not need to admire in order to love? Even at the beginning of their courtship, Inès's flirtation with any man who happened to pay her attention did not make Giacomo jealous. It struck him as alien. He understood, or made himself understand, that hers was a harmless weakness (which was a kind way of avoiding saying crassness or tastelessness).

He himself was faultlessly loyal. One would not expect anything less from Giacomo. Giacomo was loyal to Inès as much for Inès's sake as for his own – or, let us put it this way: to Giacomo, respect for others was one and the same with his *amour-propre*.

At each instance of Inès's frivolous distraction, Giacomo had been mildly disgusted but tolerated it with largesse. One rainy afternoon, coming home to see Inès in bed with her lover, his whole being was sickened, but more by the fact that, knowing full well her weakness, he had himself consciously made her his life choice.

It was not that Giacomo lacked the strength to break with Inès. He lacked the ire and vehemence to negate his own decision.

For all his decisions, Giacomo assumed full responsibility. Come what may, loyal he remained.

11

Unlike Giacomo, Mark could not love someone for whom he had no admiration. From the moment he knew Rosanna he admired her. He admired her clarity of thought, her guileless luminosity, her noble impulse. His love kept deepening, even after her death. That no woman could re-enact or replace the admiration he felt for Rosanna was as evident as it was irrelevant. Mark did not have notions of loyalty as such. As is the case with old-fashioned men and women of letters, words *meant* something. Years ago, at the Balliol College Chapel, looking into Rosanna's eyes, he swore: 'Till death us do part.' And that was that.

12

Staring at a fresco of pastoral bliss on his bedroom ceiling that night, Mark chewed over Giacomo's sentence: 'All this to not betray the hypothesis even when I have been betrayed.'

Barely had they sat down at the dinner table the following day when he said to Giacomo: 'Sir, you cannot betray a hypothesis. You can only invalidate it.'

'I beg your pardon?'

'Your hypothesis that love is unconditional, upon which you have based your marriage. If you do not, or do not wish to, judge the hypothesis invalid after your marriage has failed, it can only suggest that the hypothesis is to you not a hypothesis but a belief.'

Giacomo reflected for a moment, then responded: 'The success or failure of my marriage is not exclusively related to the truth or falsehood of my love. As for the hypothesis: my own action validates it, daily.'

'Then,' slowly said Mark, 'short of a circular argument, yours is an act of faith.'

'An act of faith it is.'

13

With Giacomo's faith, Mark was at home. By definition, love is an act of faith. All virtue is, in the last analysis, a hypothesis.

He looked across the large lacquer table at Giacomo. Tall, lean, unusually elegant even in his seventies, Giacomo was not the type that one would leave. So why did Inès betray him? Why did she go back to Paris? Why did she not want a divorce after thirty years?

Mark was far too discreet to ask. He had looked at Giacomo intently when he spoke, and listened carefully to his silence. In his mind he saw Inès, a blue-eyed, well-intentioned leftie from the sixties, unwittingly revolting against Giacomo's goodness. Giacomo the aristocrat was her 'class enemy' in the parlance of her youth. Yet, deep down she knew Giacomo to be a better human being, more elevated than she ever could be. Her light-hearted infidelity was her subconscious's revenge. That rainy afternoon, seeing Giacomo's devastated face, for the first time she grasped that her acts had consequences upon another soul, and felt shame. Shame compelled her to leave Florence with Lorenzo.

Mark's conjecture came eerily close to reality. When

Inès met Giacomo, she knew she had never met anyone as good as he. When they parted ways, she knew she would never meet anyone as good as he. And if she could not be faithful to him sexually, she would be faithful to him ceremonially. Telling herself that Giacomo was the love of her life, she remained his wife. This symbolic loyalty brought her peace, with which she buried her shame.

14

Vito's father worked for Giacomo's parents, then for Giacomo and Inès. When his father retired, a young Vito, a talented chef in his own right, took over the kingdom of the kitchen in the palazzo.

Vito loved his little universe. Above all, he loved Giacomo. Like Leone, the butler, Vito held an old-fangled reverence for Giacomo. Aware that Inès had a visitor from time to time, he breathed not a word. After Inès and Lorenzo left, he saw Giacomo suffer in silence, and resolved never to leave his service.

The night before the lockdown, Vito and his wife came to a decision: Vito would stay in the palazzo, and Laura, who worked as a nurse when younger, would volunteer at the Hospital of Santa Maria Nuova.

Some may find their decision courageous, selfless. But neither Laura nor Vito considered there to be an alternative. Neither would question the necessity of their decision in the days to come.

15

Giacomo had been funding factories that would make masks, and hotels that would accommodate doctors and nurses. When, ten days into the lockdown, he learned from Vito of the exhaustion of Laura and her colleagues, he suggested that meals be prepared daily at the palazzo and delivered to the hospital.

Obliging, Vito had since had Leone's help in the kitchen. They were soon joined by Mark. Giacomo would drop in and lend a hand.

Like elsewhere in the country, they would burst into song to boost morale, though shyly, in the confines of the kitchen. It was during these culinary hours that Vito and Leone would hear Mark chant Verdi in a transported state, and Mark would dance (by way of gesturing with his head and hips) to the Beatles sung by Vito and Leone with an Italian accent.

16

Leone was up since 4am. His sister had died in Turin.

Italy was in mourning. Funereal news on the national television had become hourly routine.

The velocity of it all shook Leone to the core. He had last seen his sister at Christmas. Recently retired, she had been taking life-drawing classes. Her son and his wife had had a baby. Her daughter was getting engaged.

Memories of them both as children came flooding back. Leone and Donatella grew up in Florence in the sixties, near Santa Croce. As a young girl, Donatella wanted to be an artist. But she was 'sensible' and studied finance in Milan, and married a man from Turin. Leone lived and worked all his life in Florence. Some years, when Giacomo spent the winter away, he would celebrate Christmas with Donatella and her family.

Now he remembered Donatella's wedding almost thirty years ago: friends and extended families at Santa Croce; the sweat and excitement of everyone on that midsummer's day; Donatella radiating happiness.

Leone tried to remain his stoic self as he donned his overcoat, and stepped out of his room when dawn broke.

17

Blue sky. Glorious sunshine. The cruellest month.

Mark gazed at the dome from his window.

Four weeks earlier, he had walked to Piazza del Duomo the day before the lockdown. He was the only person on the square.

Fear had become real in Italy. It had not reached England.

Mark went round and round the Duomo in a trance, like the last man on earth.

No public space had ever moved him so much. No other city had conversed with him so continually in the language of a thinking, breathing, civic ethos. That humanism could be the foundation of otherwise unthinkable achievements was every inch as concrete as the marble edifices each citizen strode past.

Never had that conversation seemed more poignant to Mark than it did in this desolate hour, on this deserted square.

18

When the Signoria of Florence decided towards the end of the thirteenth century to rebuild their cathedral, they appointed the most brilliant minds, and did so for two centuries. Giotto would die and Pisano would continue his design, notwithstanding disruptions of the Black Death. Ghiberti and Brunelleschi would compete, but collaborate. Judging immediate realities inferior, Florentines sought to revive olden virtues of chosen ancestors. Clothed in antique garments, art would be personal *ingenium* embodying a just polity. Indeed the learned and virtuous would govern. Those who governed should be learned and virtuous. By assuming the mortality of culture, they gave theirs a rebirth – albeit of something without precedence. In time, this *Rinascita* too would die, and here again we would stand.

We have been further removed from the Florentine Republic than it believed it had been from classical ideals, thought Mark. And on we would go to endure a plague, as had they.

Dusk set in. Mark stopped in front of the east doors of the Baptistery. He turned, and watched the bell tower sink into obscurity.

The prophets looked soberly back.

Two

1

Working through the archive, Mark was reminded of the handwriting of Rosanna's father when he re-read the self-criticism of the young man condemned in Wuhan.

He realised that this man was one year older than Rosanna's father, and that the two, who had equally graceful handwriting, had identical beginnings of misfortune.

What Rosanna knew about her father, she told Mark. It came to miserably little. Around the time Japan invaded China, starting the Second World War in Asia, her father was born. A child prodigy, he published poetry aged eight, when the Sino-Japanese War ended and the civil war resumed. Barely a teenager, he stayed in Beijing when his parents and brother fled to Taiwan. While at Beijing University, for defending the autonomy of professors he was labelled in the Anti-Rightist Campaign, and was sent to labour camps, then to a remote village, for twenty years. For twenty years he was condemned, until 1977, when the Cultural Revolution had come to an end and universities reopened. He returned to Beijing and to the University.

He never spoke of his past, and to Rosanna he talked about one thing and one thing only: classical Chinese literature.

2

Telling Giacomo about the archive, Mark lamented: 'A hellish situation whence there was no exit. The so-called crimes of which the intellectuals were accused, I could imagine myself committing every day. Indeed I might simply have perished had I lived then and there. He who thinks critically and who never experiences that level of oppression may consider himself lucky. And I consider myself lucky. But in an odd way, I'm not all that certain if in my own world today, that is to say the university, freedom of thought can be taken for granted.'

'I'm dismayed to hear that,' said Giacomo. 'For many here, the British education system is a model.'

'There are *still* many good things to be said about our education system.' Mark tried to sound as uncomplaining as possible as he sought to make plain what he meant, thinking about the 'five-year plans', 'impact initiatives', 'output assessments', 'partnerships with students', 'collaborations with industry', and so forth, to which academics in Britain had been subjected for about a decade: 'But as it stands, it's turning into a dysfunctioning planned economy and a soulless capitalist enterprise combined.'

3

For Mark, it had lately become difficult to think of the 'five-year plans', 'impact initiatives', 'output assessments', 'partnerships with students', 'collaborations with industry', and so forth, without recalling the slogan 'Ample, Fast, Good, Thrifty' being applied to the humanities in China in the 1950s. The same principle applied: produce, and produce quantifiable appearances, spending as little money as possible (funding would be tantamount to squander) and as little time as possible (Research? Time? What nonsense!). The young man in Wuhan was right sixty years ago: research couldn't be good if it were ample, fast and thrifty. Had he worked in a British university today he wouldn't have a great time. He wouldn't be persecuted, that's for sure, but neither would he flourish.

'How do planned economy and capitalist enterprise combine in higher education?' asked Giacomo.

How do they combine? Mark thought to himself: University administration manages academics with Soviet strategies, obliging academics to function – even to think or write – like bureaucrats to survive. Applying for research funding, one must delineate the outcome of one's exploration (in advance) and the significance of it (as if it were for oneself to say). Copying their American counterparts, universities in England are now businesses, only without the funds necessary to run them, governmental support having declined since the financial crisis. Universities are thus enterprises without money, taking themselves for sellers of qualification and students for purchasers of their goods. Students, paying enormous fees, take themselves for customers and education as commodity. Academics, overworked and poorly paid, are made to justify themselves constantly to management, well-paid by contrast, and to promote themselves on the education market. It is humiliating. It is humiliation sold as pride. Those who are brave leave. Those who stay languish.

But all this is humiliating even to recount, thought Mark. Instead he replied: 'Fascinates me too. Suffice to say: an anti-intellectual executive is running an anti-education system. Curious marriage; and a defining feature of our post-Cold War reality.'

'Makes one rethink the Cold War premises,' said Giacomo. 'Before passing verdict, one might concede that no society is perfect, or could ever be; neither the communist dream turned nightmare, nor the capitalist free world turned hostage.'

4

Still thinking about Giacomo's comment, Mark asked him the next day: 'Sir, do you remember where you were when the Wall fell?'

'Yes. I was at home, and saw it on the news. In the seventies I spent three months in West Berlin; the Wall was standing then.'

'What was it like?'

'Unsettling. I mean West Berlin. I shouldn't have been disappointed by Germany – after all, I have loved Goethe, Kleist, and Nietzsche since adolescence, speak German and love what you might call German high culture, the music and all – but I was. Disappointed.'

'Why?'

'Berlin... is a city without form,' Giacomo put it across apologetically, with a rueful smile and reiteration for emphasis. 'It is an ugly, formless city. And I am sorry for judging it aesthetically. But seriously, what we call German high culture has practically nothing to do with Germany as a country. I have kept my admiration for the music and the literature – the greatest of it – and remain unimpressed by the country till this day, reunited or not.'

'But that's the point,' said Mark. 'Germany was not a nation-state until a century and a half ago, and even this patchwork of a country has since gone through more divisions and transmutations than we care to acknowledge. We so often assume things and people to be homogenous.'

'Indeed. Generalisations make only dubious sense, and I'm biased on many accounts, but you know what I mean when I say that Merkel, for example, is almost un-German. To me she is a fair-minded, big-hearted Christian with an outmoded public spirit.'

'I know what you mean,' concurred Mark. 'For many in Britain, Merkel stood as the leader of liberal Europe during the refugee crisis. In Germany, support for her plummeted during the same crisis. Not so liberal after all. Last November I happened to be in Berlin. On the thirtieth anniversary of the fall, as evening came, I took a walk along the former Wall. It was grim. Dismal. Some people tried to dance near the Brandenburger Tor; most just drank; empty beer cans were left everywhere on the street; a cheerless mob. After the Wall fell, Berlin experienced a golden age of sorts, at least in popular myth. But at bottom it remains a poor city as it always has been, with an underlying despair. Near midnight, I took a taxi back to my hotel, and asked the driver how he felt about the reunification. He was from the East. He hated it then, and he hated it now. You know, I do not think I have ever seen a city more desperately discordant, more in ruinous disharmony with everything and with itself.'

'Then we understand each other.' Giacomo looked at Mark, his eyes beaming with recognition.

5

After Rosanna died, Mark read in her journal an entry from 21 July 1999. 'Ten years ago, on this day, in the afternoon I came home to find father sitting at his desk in the study, his back to the door, his head in his hands. Struck by his stillness, I stood at the door for a long time, unable to utter a sound. I saw a man in agony. His hair had gone completely white that summer – now I know why. He was appalled by what had happened at Tiananmen. Mother wanted to leave. He wanted to stay. They argued. Their argument sounded like a long heartbreaking plea. Tears were shed. That was the last time I saw him. That evening, mother and I left.'

Rosanna had not shared with Mark this memory. Perhaps it was too sad to recollect. Perhaps meeting Mark later made her forget.

She had forgotten how to speak Chinese, but not how to write. Until the age of ten, she had learned the language most of all as a written one, reading classical prose and poetry with her father each afternoon – it was their only real communication. In those studious hours, she felt her father to be content, more at peace than at any other time.

6

'The only thing I have inherited from my father', Rosanna once told Mark, 'is an attachment to his language in its ancient form. At times I wonder if it's the only thing alive in him. Or the only thing that sustains him.'

Both as a child and later as an adult, Rosanna looked upon her father as someone peering over a fortress and trying to conjure up what was inside.

'I am saddened thinking of you growing up with a father so guarded,' Mark said to Rosanna.

Rosanna said nothing. Having each of us only one father, one could hardly imagine how things might have been different.

She was more sorry thinking of her father being guarded. Even as a small child, she had understood that emotional armour was the sign of a wound.

By way of responding, she told Mark what, aged fourteen, she had asked her mother on the phone: 'What attracted you to Dad?'

'What did your Mum say?' asked Mark.

'That he was a most handsome man. And most melancholy.'

Mark nearly laughed. The incoming laughter turned forthwith into a sigh.

The answer of Rosanna's mother said more about her than about her husband.

Rosanna's mother followed only her heart. First, she studied art against her parents' will. Then she married a man without her parents' approval. After eleven years of marriage in Beijing, she returned to London, and saw an inevitable end to her ten-year child-rearing: now her daughter stood to remind her of her failed rebellion. She left Rosanna with her parents, and continued her revolt on a different path.

7

Rosanna's mother was understood by her daughter alone.

When Mark and Rosanna decided to marry, she declined their wedding invitation.

That day, Rosanna cried. Sobbing in Mark's arms, she murmured softly: 'She resented me for her disillusioned youth. It was better that I be out of sight. She brought me back with her. She did what she could. It is not her fault.'

Mark held her very tight. He could not understand how parents could be so cruel and a child so kind. He could not understand Rosanna's will to forgive.

8

Rosanna forgave her parents, for she loved them. She loved as a child loves and wants to be loved: unconditionally.

She remembered the romantic existences of her parents in Beijing. Their cosmopolitan, multilingual circle of friends. Their ardent discussions of art and literature late into the night. Their high-minded discourse of politics that a little Rosanna struggled to comprehend.

Above all, she remembered their naïveté and innocence. Rosanna's father had been traumatised by his country. But he believed that the trauma had had its end. Rosanna's mother would discover trauma later – at which point her husband's hair turned white overnight.

When Mark had learned to read Chinese, he read the fifteen letters Rosanna had received from her father. All short, all distant; the last, written upon learning that Rosanna was expecting a child, amounted to a curse. 'You are wrecking your career by having a child so early,' he wrote, 'you will live to regret this.'

Mark was furious.

He penned a strongly worded letter, and sent it

to the address in Beijing. He told Rosanna's father (seeing the latter had no idea) of his daughter's obvious fragility and fortitude, of her brilliance and independence, of her empathy and consideration for others; and questioned his father-in-law's very act of cruelty and lack of humanity in the face of the defencelessness and graciousness of another human being.

A reply came six months later, ten pages long. Rosanna's father bemoaned the loss of his daughter and explained why he had said what he had said in his last letter, upholding his good intentions but conceding that he was nonetheless wrong, et cetera.

Mark was singularly unmoved by this lengthy atonement. A nameless pity overcame his fury. For a very long time, he did not understand why.

He never replied.

9

Now, more than a decade having passed, the self-criticism of the young man in Wuhan awakened Mark's memories of this letter from Beijing.

It dawned on him that it was the same kind of

confession, the same kind of language, and the same kind of disingenuousness, almost certainly involuntary: the letter, like the self-criticism, was self-reproach that sounded like self-defence, remorse that verged on apathy.

Only then did Mark recognise the extent of the old man's trauma. Only then could he name the nameless pity he had felt all those years ago, reading the letter.

So this was what twenty years' defiance of persecution had come down to: a permanent topsy-turvy camouflage in deliberation; a cold streak in the human heart.

10

What I know now by analysis, thought Mark, Rosanna had known by intuition.

In life as in work, Rosanna took for granted the mystery of the human soul. With wonder she regarded history as she did people. Mark recalled her saying that 1989 ought to be studied as global history – 'Those on the streets of Prague were aware of what had happened in Beijing.' He delighted in her capacity for thinking in juxtaposition: quoting Petrarch, she would cite Confucius, and in such a way as to betray that she saw them as her friends.

One evening, Mark said to Giacomo: 'Sir, I think you would have enjoyed talking to my late wife.'

'Tell me about her, Mark,' said Giacomo ever so gently.

'She was the most gifted scholar I knew, yet unassuming. She loved Greek and Latin as much as she did ancient Chinese. And spoke French as well as she did Italian. The only person I knew who took equal pleasure in reading a Nabokov novel and the first edition of the Larousse.' Mark smiled, as he saw in his mind Rosanna's concentrated expression when she devoured dictionaries.

'A Renaissance person. And you miss her,' said Giacomo, tenderness in his voice.

'I do.' Mark's eyes became moist as he looked smilingly at Giacomo. 'Terribly.'

11

Mark loved Rosanna so much that, had he been able to die in her place, he would have. Were he able to bring her back in exchange of his own life, he would do so.

Rosanna remained his closest friend. In spirit, he had continued their conversation. In the Republic of Letters, all is dead, and all is living.

When Mark woke up in the middle of the night, his first instinct was still to find Rosanna breathing tranquilly by his side.

And his arms were empty.

12

The day after he spoke to Giacomo about Rosanna, Mark showed him the young man's dossier in the archive: a summary of his crimes handwritten by the authorities, and numerous piles of self-criticism, from 1957 to 1959, written on paper that bore the official imprint: 'University of Wuhan'.

As they looked at the first self-criticism from 24 September 1957, Mark translated for Giacomo the first page:

'What I would like to tell everyone first of all, is how I came to be anti-party and anti-socialist. The full answer is to be set in context. In short, I started by doubting the Party, then my political position wavered, and I ended up being anti-party. Indeed I am an Enemy of the People. I am a henchman of the rightists. I have committed a crime against the People. Please see the following for details.

'First: reactionary family situation. The sin of my father. In the past, I only considered my father and myself to be two different people, and that his wickedness had nothing to do with me. I thought that, as long as I did not cover his crimes, and spoke to and contacted him little, it would be fine and I, following the Party, would not be in the wrong. If you thought of it, that wasn't so bad! But it wasn't that simple. My heart and soul were inextricably linked to this family, and I could not get over it emotionally. (I always felt that, at his now advanced age, physical labour – blacksmithing – was a bit too much. Wasn't life more comfortable before? So I had sympathy for him… Especially as I heard people say that when he was in the internment camp he was often made to kneel on bricks or even beaten up, I held a slight grudge against the Party for it: he never killed anyone, and had even joined the National Revolutionary Army of the Republic of China, once almost losing his life – persecuting him thus was rather overkill. What abominable class sympathy on my part!) I must have instinctively demonstrated this feeling, even though

I never confided it to anyone. This feeling indeed induced in me a resentment towards the Party, it constantly stopped me from accepting new things, and so I could not develop a deeper understanding of the Party. Under the circumstances, it was not for no reason that I committed a crime against the People. Please refer to my usual arrogant behaviour and my reactionary opinions during the "Free Airing of Views Movement" for further proof.'

Giacomo was aghast. He looked closely at the pages, feeling them in his hands. 'Why was his father placed in internment?' he asked.

Mark turned to the official summary of the young man's crimes, and said: 'His father had worked for the Japanese-supported collaborationist government in Nanjing during the Second World War. After the communists came to power in 1949, he was held in internment camp for three years. By 1957, he had been working as a blacksmith for the commune.'

Visibly touched, Giacomo said nothing more. He thanked Mark, and bade him good evening before retiring for the night.

13

The next morning, Giacomo came to see Mark in his study.

'I didn't sleep much last night, Mark.' He walked slowly to the window, which framed a centuries-old skyline against a blue azure. After a minute he turned, looking sad: 'There are the monstrous implications of the crippling consequences of oppression, of extreme political movements throughout the last century. And there are the difficult relations between humans, between generations, that are still more difficult in a political tourbillon.'

Upright, Mark offered Giacomo the only chair in the space. Giacomo remained standing. 'Nearly half a century ago', he said, 'in this room, I stumbled upon amicable letters that my father had received from fascist officials throughout the thirties.'

'Was your father...?'

'No. He may have had fascist sympathies, but was not involved in any actual way.'

'Did you speak about it?'

'We did. To be sure, he had reproachable friendships. But from what I could find out, nothing less and nothing more. I remember standing here in this room, looking out the window, deciding not to judge him for it. It was not a decision that ignored moral questions. It *was* a moral decision. For one has the right to keep one's friends. If he did not personally do anything wrong, who am I to judge him? At most I may disapprove of his taste in friendship, but no more. You see, what struck me yesterday, when you showed me the young man's self-criticism, was that he was forced to judge his father by those who had no business judging neither father nor son. The young man said, rightly, that his father never killed anyone – there was no legal guilt; nor moral responsibility, as far as I can see. When political interests override legality in the name of morality, a totalitarian regime can be identified: the state acts as though it were God, with the divine right to judge everyone.'

'Thinking carefully to determine *whether* to judge and *how* to judge – this in itself is judgement; it is an act too little exercised. Throughout the last century, sons were busy judging their fathers,' said Mark, 'and hastily.'

'This careless judging of what precedes us,' agreed Giacomo, 'I'm afraid began earlier, metaphorically speaking. In Europe, it culminated in the French Revolution, and never ceased culminating in revolutions since. The entire nineteenth century was a struggle against revolutions and consequences of revolutions. In the twentieth century, communist and fascist movements alike carried the name of revolution, red or black. And after each judgemental revolution came post-revolution judgements, no less forbidding.'

Mark suspired. 'What was destroyed, in the name of justice, was not inequality, nor poverty, nor class, nor menace to the nation, but moral common sense.'

Giacomo stared at him: 'Do such persuasions not make you unpopular amongst academics today?'

'Certainly,' answered Mark with solemnity. 'For twenty years I've been accused of being a reactionary.'

14

The difference between conservatism and reactionism is a monumental one. If a definition must be given, Mark would consider himself a conservative, one who appreciated equivalently liberal and progressive ideas, provided that they be not extreme.

But now and again, some self-proclaimed progressives classified him as from an adverse camp – such was the zeal for classifications and for camps.

It probably would have been feasible to masquerade as being in the same clique, to save the hassle. But Mark had difficulty singing the same song. Over time, he assumed an amiable silence during group meetings and discussions.

Without taking it personally, Mark saw his being misunderstood as part and parcel of a general fading of healthy conservatism in the thinking world.

Now he knew that, during the Anti-Rightist Campaign, many who were labelled Enemies of the People were simply conservative, or indeed liberal, or even overwhelmingly progressive. Few, however, learned to be silent (or had the luxury to learn it). Most of them were trusting. Almost all were outspoken – more so, thought Mark, than himself; more so, thought he, than the majority of his colleagues today.

15

'I sympathise,' said Giacomo. 'Intellectuals are supposed to make known their reasoning. Yet they pay a price for doing so.'

Mark heaved a sigh. Between the awkward situation in which he and his colleagues found themselves, one-fifth into the twenty-first century, and the mass persecution of thinking beings everywhere in the twentieth, a lot needed to be understood.

He too walked towards the window, which framed a centuries-old skyline against an azure almost indigo. Standing next to Giacomo, he said: 'That price was unbearable at times. It had meant one's career. It had meant one's life. At best, it left one half dead deep in one's soul. But if the price was free speech, all might not be lost. The vital point is not to lose reasoning itself – or the ability to love.'

Three

1

Mid-April. The lockdown had been prolonged.

Mark set out to translate a small selection of documents from the archive.

'Would you like to read it in English or in Italian, sir?'

'Your choice, Mark. In English, if you might use it later for publication?' said Giacomo.

Looking at the dossiers he had set aside, Mark saw not material for publication, but people with whom he would rather have a conversation.

'Like you, sir, I am concerned with the individuals.' Mark rested his hand gently on a dusty pile of old paper. 'The destinies of these men and women have most affected me. I have tried to find out if some of them may still be alive.'

He opened a yellowing envelope. 'This file was issued by the authorities in Shanghai. How did it end up in the Wuhan municipal archive? I have no clue. We have here an official report from the 14th of September 1970, along with witness accounts, on a Shanghai artist. It looks as though he later immigrated to Macau in 1982, and works there as an artist to this day.'

'What was his alleged crime?'

'Anti-party opinions, which did not land him in

trouble during the Anti-Rightist Campaign, possibly because no one reported him, but which came back to haunt him in 1970, when acquaintances were made to recount what he'd said a decade earlier. Several recalled the remarks he'd made – for instance: "The Chinese Communist Party's proposal of 'long-term coexistence and mutual supervision' is a sham. They are, in every form and shape, a one-party dictatorship. It is by deceit that they have shot down democrats during this Anti-Rightist Campaign. It is thus that many talents have been crushed."'

'He said that out loud? And saw things so clearly?'

'Absolutely. Reported by third parties or in their own accounts, nearly all the accused had left nothing unexamined, nothing unsaid. It was truth at all cost,' said Mark with emotion.

'Remarkable,' muttered Giacomo indistinctly. 'How old was he?'

'Same age as the young man from Wuhan. Twenty-one during the Anti-Rightist Campaign. Thirty-four when this file was made – four years into the Cultural Revolution.'

'I see. Do we know what happened to the young man in Wuhan during the Cultural Revolution?'

'No.'

2

When Giacomo asked again if he might like to travel to China to learn more about the figures in the archive, Mark was curiously uneager.

Later, he told Giacomo about Rosanna's father. 'As I try to understand the existential conditions of those in the dossiers, my thoughts keep going back to him. Beyond the superficial parallels, there are hard questions I struggle to answer.'

Mark was by then in no doubt of his father-in-law's forthright opinion-voicing, in like manner as his counterparts in the archive, during the Anti-Rightist Campaign. And he ended up wondering:

Telling one's pregnant daughter that she's ruining her life by having a child is humanly unacceptable: one may think so but not say so. Could it be the defence mechanism of the persecuted – might it be the almost destructive impulse of Truth at All Cost – that made Rosanna's father write as he did? In other words, could it be his *lifelong reflex to say precisely what he thought?* Like a veteran soldier at never-ending war, he acted out a drawn-out duel with systemic falsehood.

Only his daughter's life was not a system of falsehood. In that never-ending duel he fought – now real, now figmental – courtesy was but a secondary consideration. Truth at all cost.

3

Hearing Mark unveil his innermost thoughts, Giacomo implored: 'My boy, I'm heartbroken. If you would allow me – wouldn't you like to meet your father-in-law, and talk to him?'

Mark was torn. Too much stood between him and Rosanna's father. Too much history, unwritten. Too much grief, unspoken.

He looked gravely at Giacomo, and replied: 'No, sir. I don't think so.'

4

The question of moral measure, that of *whether* and *how* to judge, sat centrally in Mark's mind.

I understand you now, he longed to say to Rosanna, wiping away her tears, I now share your will to forgive. But I do not want my compassion to be a self-indulgent act of charity, undeserved; nor a self-serving act of clemency, misplaced. Tell me, Rosanna, would it make a difference, if I knew your father?

5

It did not take Mark long to deduce that his father-in-law might be alive. A poet of some renown, he was widely read in the eighties. If he died, one would know.

For all that, there appeared to be no news of him since the last collection of his poetry was published, in 2007.

Delicately persistent, Giacomo said: 'Mark, it is neither indifference nor disinterest that makes you reluctant, I think. If I may, I guess you are apprehensive for both probable outcomes of an eventual encounter with Rosanna's father: that you come to like him; that you in fact loathe him.'

'That may be right, sir.' In a grateful tone, Mark added: 'And the fear that wounds in both hearts be reopened.'

6

Giacomo did not insist.

A week later, when he came to the kitchen to lend Vito a hand, Mark and Leone, washing and peeling vegetables, were engaged in a discussion.

'Signore,' asked Leone, 'what do you think of the theory that Covid-19 came from a lab in Wuhan?'

'As things stand,' Mark paused to greet Giacomo with a smile, 'there is no evidence supporting it. And there is no apparent motive. Last but not least, since January, scientists have studied the virus's sequence and reckoned it originated in nature. So the question is: Since when do we not give a damn about science?'

That happened to be a discussion Giacomo himself had just had. 'Without evidence and against science,' he said, 'it leaves suspicion of motive to be driving the theory.'

When a former colleague of Giacomo's phoned from Paris that morning, he said he suspected the virus to be man-made. Giacomo replied that it was, scientifically speaking, impossible. The colleague then said a virus from nature *accidentally* got out of the lab. One cannot exclude accident as a probability, said Giacomo, but for that accident to happen, an unknown virus would first need to be discovered, collected, and stored in the research institute – whose job it was to make known any such discoveries – without anyone knowing it, which would be implausible, and nobody would have anything to gain from it. His colleague laughed, and said Giacomo was being naïve.

Naïve, or rational? In the tenacity of his colleague's suspicion, Giacomo saw his need to locate a root cause of our present misfortune. The scientists' inference that some animal transmitted the disease did not satisfy that need – the need for a villain.

7

All day long, Giacomo thought about what he had read the night before.

Mark had given him the translation of a dossier: 'On the envelope that contains the fate of this young woman, it is written: "Dead".'

'What was the cause of her death?'

'Nowhere indicated. Born in Jakarta to a Chinese father and an Indonesian mother, as a teenager she wanted to study in China. Her father, a successful entrepreneur, granted her wish in 1953. She attended high schools in Shanghai before being admitted to the Wuhan Medical College in 1958. This file consists mainly of self-evaluations and of evaluations by the authorities: high schools, the university, the labour force she joined, and the Ministry of Education.'

'What were the evaluations for?'

'In keeping with the changing political wind, periodic evaluations were the norm around 1957. By then, anyone dubious would have had a file; those with overseas connections were under extra scrutiny.'

'And why the labour force?'

'In imitation of the Soviet "Saturday voluntary labour" programme, university students began working in fields or in factories in the mid-fifties. Their physical labour intensified in 1957, in conjunction with the Anti-Rightist Campaign; then with the Great Leap Forward from 1958 to 1960, years when she was at the College.'

Later that evening, Giacomo read, inter alia, two letters dated November and December 1958. The first was written by the girl's father in Jakarta, and addressed to the chairwoman of the Overseas Chinese Affairs Committee. The Committee in Beijing forwarded his letter to the Wuhan Medical College, recommending considered action. The second was sent by the chairman of the Jakarta Association of Overseas Chinese to the Wuhan Medical College. Both conveyed the same message: the girl had fallen ill while doing physical labour, suffering headaches, vomiting often, and coughing blood. Her weight had dropped from fifty-five to forty-five kilos. The doctor prescribed rest, but it was not allowed by her team leader, who derided her capitalist background. Her father beseeched the authorities to let her return to health before resuming her contribution to the great socialist project.

The College assumably took the Committee's advice and eased her workload. By 1960 she was well and married to a fellow medical student.

The last document, dated 18 January 1962, was a form issued by the Ministry of Education – she had finished her studies and was waiting to be allocated work. It was half-completed. She had left blank the section of self-evaluation, and the university did not bother evaluating her work prospects, leaving that section also blank. On the last page, an official hand had filled out the section of political evaluation, stating that other than connections with her family abroad, she was unproblematic.

If the word 'Dead' on her file summed up what occurred thereafter, thought Giacomo, she would have died before being allocated work, and before turning twenty-six years old.

8

One detail stayed with Giacomo: the girl's self-evaluations.

The first was written when she was at No. 56 High School of Shanghai. Her merits, she wrote, were 'a love of art: dance, musical instruments, the fine arts; and an interest in biology'; and her shortcomings, 'a weak will and a short temper'.

After three years at the Wuhan Medical College, she listed her merits as: '(1) I am docile, I listen to the Party, and wish to be progressive politically; (2) I can accept criticism and correct my shortcomings; (3) I am hardworking when it comes to physical labour; (4) I am responsible in my work, and mobilise all my resources to complete tasks; (5) I participate in Criticism and Self-criticism; (6) I side with the Party, seek help from the Party when necessary, and regard the Party as my family; (7) I fight against all harmful phenomena in my own bourgeois family.

As for her shortcomings, she wrote: '(1) I harbour individualism in my thinking, a weak will, and a lack of self-discipline; (2) I sometimes don't follow closely institutional instructions; (3) I am not sufficiently keen to join the Youth League; (4) I have a short temper, and when confronting things I fail to stay calm.'

In 1958, upon entering the university she had written an 'autobiography' on request, and candidly told: As the eldest child of her parents, she saw her mother suffer when her father took a second wife, then a third. The desire to defend her mother, to stand up for the helpless, defined her childhood: hence her hot temper; hence her resolve to become an independent person working in a progressive society like the People's Republic of China, where women had equal opportunities, made their own living, and were respected.

That's why she went to China, said Giacomo to himself, and why she stayed on even though, as the case may be, she could have left. But returning to Indonesia was not an option: Jakarta was never her home. Neither, it would seem, was Wuhan.

9

Mark and Giacomo exchanged a dejected look as they sat down that evening.

'Hers, sir, was not an isolated case.'

'I imagined as such, Mark.'

'Thousands of second-generation Chinese-Indonesians went to China in the fifties and sixties, to study to become engineers and doctors. They went for patriotic reasons. They went voluntarily. Some disappeared. Some later appeared in Hong Kong as refugees.'

'And this girl?' Giacomo looked at the envelope sealed by the word 'Dead'. 'I still can't get over the fact that a full human life came down to this, a pile of papers. And ended up half a century later, thousands of miles away, on a desk.'

'I know,' said Mark. 'In my wishful thinking, she had somehow feigned her death, and managed to reach Hong Kong and live a peaceful, fulfilled life.'

'Wouldn't that be nice!' whispered Giacomo.

10

Mark could only surmise the odds played in those hysterical Cold War years against Rosanna's father, whose family had chosen Taiwan, by then an enemy regime. He began to think of his father-in-law's very survival as a miracle.

'The file I am translating now', said he to Giacomo, 'is that of a chemistry student. At seventeen, he was labelled a rightist in his first year at the University of Wuhan. The last document in his file was dated four years later, when he'd finished his studies: a proposal from the Party's general branch committee of the University's Chemistry Department to remove his rightist label.'

'Why had he been labelled?'

'He had asserted, and his classmates reported, that the Soviet suppression of the 1956 Hungarian Uprising was a violation of international law; that Stalin was a monster who killed hundreds of thousands in 1937 and that the Chinese Communist Party was making the same mistake; that a socialist democracy as claimed in China ought to make available foreign newspapers; and that had the great leftist writer, Lu Xun, admired by Mao, lived in the present, he'd have been labelled a rightist and imprisoned.'

'In effect, intellectuals across the Eastern Bloc had shared concerns at the time.'

'Beyond a doubt.'

'And all these views from a seventeen-year-old!'

'Indeed. After this, he seemed to have done all that was required, be it physical labour or self-criticism.

But comrades reported his resentment, as revealed by his reaction when injured at work. Pointing to his bleeding leg, they asked if it hurt, and he replied: "I'm numb. How can one not be numb after being labelled a rightist?"'

'Did the proposal to remove his label meet with a conclusion?' asked Giacomo.

'Not as far as his file shows. Here's the peculiar thing: his name is written on the back of an envelope that has someone else's name and profession on the front – a lecturer in Economics. And this envelope in turn is placed in another, which bears the lecturer's name and is marked: "Dead".'

'So we don't know what happened to the chemistry student. We know this economics lecturer was dead.'

'That's right.'

'And the file of the lecturer is not in his envelope.'

'That's exact.'

11

In all probability, Mark suggested to Giacomo, these deaths were casualties of the Great Famine, itself a consequence of the failed Great Leap Forward.

What was difficult to make sense of, for Mark, was the senselessness of it all. A revolution declared an autocrat a saviour; the saviour, starting to fear for his power, launched one movement after another in the name of utopia. Unspeakable miseries befell a nation for a quarter of a century.

Why did it happen? Why did it happen in the face of good consciences and free spirits everywhere in the country? Who was responsible for these deaths? Who was responsible for the pointless sacrifice of several generations of youths?

Destruction on this colossal scale was altogether criminal. Could anyone be held accountable? Is there, indeed, a villain?

12

Mark tried to picture the circumstances of the girl from Jakarta. He thought about the team leader who did not allow her to rest. Might he or she have been under pressure? Undoubtedly. Might he or she have themselves suffered? Most certainly. In that respect, he or she was not all that different from the girl from Jakarta, who had succumbed to the same pressure and had produced, as noted in one of her self-evaluations in 1959, three hundred denunciation posters in one year.

In a society that dreamt collectively of utopia, having barely recovered from a century of wars and commotion, nearly everyone who dreamt erred; nearly everyone was a victim.

But if everyone was a victim, no one would be responsible. The notion of responsibility would lose its meaning.

His or her own suffering notwithstanding, the team leader did have a choice to act differently, that is to say humanely, toward others.

13

In the same year that the girl unwillingly wrote three hundred denunciation posters, tens of thousands went to prison for not conforming to the demands of the time. Tens of thousands committed suicide to preserve their integrity.

Once more, Mark found himself wondering what he would have done under like conditions.

Woe in his heart, he looked at Giacomo, whose face under the lamplight was pensive and noble.

'Not to do wrong when doing wrong appears the only thing possible', concluded Mark, 'must be the ultimate test of humanity.'

A long silence brooded in the room before Giacomo said: 'One has to agree with Socrates: it is better to suffer wrong than to do wrong. But dear God, how desperately unjust its implication could be!'

14

Our notions of justice and responsibility are intrinsically related. Where injustice takes place, we want to know who is responsible.

Earlier that day, when Leone asked Mark about the origin of the virus, he had evoked the memory of the ophthalmologist Li Wenliang.

Any decent person would regret that the doctor who had warned of a new virus could not, while on duty, protect himself from it. The fact that he was silenced after sharing his warning made his death – at the age of thirty-four, leaving his unborn son an orphan – still harder to take.

It was unjust. And if the passing of Li Wenliang, and that of many more, could have been prevented, who should answer for it?

Local officials who had charged Doctor Li with spreading rumours were duly punished by the central government, who for their part wasted little time in recognising Wuhan's error, correcting it with draconian measures nationwide, and decorating Li Wenliang with the highest honour.

One could only do so much, you may say. This, indeed, was the view of Vito. Characteristically generous, he said to Mark and Leone: 'We are all in this together. Everywhere the virus caught us unprepared in the same way. And it attacks our bodies in the same way. Plague plagues humans. It's not the first time, and won't be the last.' Indeed, the majority of governments had only half-heartedly reacted, even when they knew what was going on; even as they saw what was unfolding in China and Italy and what was coming.

15

The question remained: Could the pandemic have been averted had Doctor Li not been shushed?

Those who suppressed truth in a bureaucratic reflex,

at a time when the World Health Organisation had been informed and Doctor Li's message had been heard: Had they understood what was at stake, would they have acted the same?

Incidentally, Mark had seen an interview of the punished official, who with his mask over his mouth and his hands in the air trying to explain his action, looked immensely panicked, immensely sorry.

Was someone guilty if they had done wrong unknowingly, out of ignorance?

Could someone be pardoned if the wrong they had done wasn't the direct, nor exclusive, cause of further affliction?

'It's getting better now in Wuhan,' said Vito. 'It will get better here.'

'Yes,' said Leone. 'It will get better.'

Touched by the valiance of Leone and Vito, Mark thought with a heavy heart: Here, each night in lockdown we applaud to thank our doctors. Seventy-seven nights ago, locked-down citizens of Wuhan kept their lights on all night long, and sang to grieve over a doctor whose truth had not spared him his life.

16

In this spring, more borders were closed than there had been in half a century. In this spring, more than half of earthlings stayed unmoving watching the stars and the television. In this spring, from pole to pole the sky was bluer than many had ever seen.

When Italy came out of lockdown, summer was waiting.

Mark and Giacomo stood wordless on Piazza della Signoria, basking in its buoyancy. More restrained than usual, its buoyancy was quietly indomitable.

'Civic pride etched in stone', slowly pronounced Giacomo, 'strikes me each time I pass here. One of the things that have not changed.'

'Ever since your youth?'

'Ever since my youth.'

Giacomo had a long memory. In history, where others saw change, he saw continuity.

An affinity with his grandfather had early set the tone. A one-time student of Philosophy in late Victorian England and the nephew of a Risorgimento figure, Giacomo's grandfather personified cultural conservatism and liberal patriotism. Giacomo's father was quite unlike his own father and son. This dissimilarity disturbed all three of them very little: their lineage was the living fusion of singularity and unity.

That was why, perhaps, Giacomo's relation to the world was distinguished by a confidence in kinship despite difference; a search for harmony through variance.

That was why, perhaps, the Wuhan archive had rattled him so. 'What I have come to terms with reading your translation', he said to Mark, 'is a sense of rupture in every direction. Radical uprooting rendered each person powerless. Life's vital references – family, friends – were negated, dismantled, regardless of people's innate goodness.'

17

Under the Florentine sun so cherished by him and Rosanna, Mark mulled over Giacomo's reflection on uprootedness. His thoughts turned again to Rosanna's father, who was only a child when his family left for Taiwan. Why did he not leave with his parents and brother? Why, forty years later, did he not leave with his wife and child for England?

'Effectively,' said Giacomo, 'your father-in-law was left an orphan, and may have been in internal exile ever since.'

'I think so. My wife believed her father's only anchor to be his language, even when that very language changed dramatically. You may recall that one of the alleged crimes of the young man in Wuhan was his criticism of the Party's language policy. A change so violent could conceivably make one's own language an alibi and an existential fight. For a poet, such a fight may even be the only thing tangible when everything else tumbles down.'

'Which could be why he would not leave his battlefield behind?' speculated Giacomo.

18

Mark had speculated along similar lines. At long last, he joined Rosanna in her empathic speculation. His consolation was amplified by Giacomo's empathy.

As they turned on to Via dei Gondi, Mark saw Giacomo smile.

'I remember the last time my grandfather and I had a drink with some friends,' said Giacomo, looking ahead.

The memory of his grandfather's cadenced reasoning on current events, and of his kindly twinkle in the eye, made Giacomo happy.

His grandfather died when Giacomo was twenty. Their loving rapport, undiminished by the distance of half a century, still meant everything to Giacomo. It meant, above all, a sense of moral belonging.

This, perhaps, is what it means to be rooted, thought Giacomo, as he felt in his gut that Rosanna's father might never have had such a rapport – one which was denied him, and which he then denied his daughter.

'Promise me, Mark,' said Giacomo warmly, 'that you will come back and visit me whenever you can.'

'I will, sir,' responded Mark with certainty.

Four

1

Seven weeks passed. One morning, Giacomo received a phone call from Mark.

'All well here, sir. I stayed two weeks quarantined in my parents' conservatory, getting acquainted with their plants; then spent time with the family; and returned to Oxford, went to the office last week. In my pigeonhole was a letter from my father-in-law.'

'From Beijing?'

'No, from Paris.'

'What did he say?'

'He said the virus was serious, and asked me to be careful. He wrote it on the 2nd of February. As I was on sabbatical, I wasn't there when it arrived.'

'I see. This is the first time you've heard from him since…'

'Since twelve years ago.'

Giacomo was as surprised as Mark. 'Did he say anything more?'

'It's a brief note. Just a warning, and a simple sentence: I think often of your letter – please forgive me, my child.'

'Extraordinary,' said Giacomo after a thoughtful pause. 'Do you…?'

'Yes. I tried to write him a letter. But it wouldn't do. You see, I have too many questions.'

'I understand.'

After a moment of stillness, Mark said matter-of-factly: 'I shall go to see him in Paris.'

'That's good of you, Mark.'

'Thank you, sir. The thing is: I see no alternative, not anymore. With your understanding, I have felt stronger. And Paris is not Beijing.'

'I'm with you. Do you think he'll be at the address from which he wrote?'

'I'll find out.'

2

Before leaving, Mark visited Lorenzo and his wife Eilidh.

Not yet forty and already into his third marriage, at first glance Lorenzo was the flip side of Giacomo.

'My father told me you were going to Paris. I thought I had to see you before you went.' Lorenzo beamed with enthusiasm, pouring Mark a glass.

'It's good to see you, Lorenzo. How was the lockdown for you and Eilidh?'

'Luckily we have this wee garden, so we can't complain.'

In their small and fragrant garden, the three academics now sat. Lorenzo continued: 'My father said his lockdown was immeasurably enriched by your presence.'

'As was mine, by his!'

'I'm so glad. He didn't mention why you were going to Paris, though. But first things first: Do you plan to self-isolate upon arrival? Have you found a place to stay?'

'Yes, I do prefer to behave properly; and no, not yet.'

'Why don't you stay at my apartment? I haven't been there much since my student days. There you can isolate yourself as long as you wish.'

'That's very kind of you, Lorenzo.'

3

It did not escape Mark's attention that Lorenzo had adopted some of Eilidh's vocabulary. Scotland was dear to Mark's heart (not least since he and Rosanna were both one-eighth Scottish); and whenever he heard Eilidh speak, it brought him joy.

Presently, Eilidh evoked Oriel College's vote on removing the Rhodes statue, the latest debate on campus that Mark had missed. Siding with the majority of their students, she and Lorenzo were satisfied with the vote, especially in view of the Black Lives Matter protests, and after the toppling of the Colston statue in Bristol.

Mark approved wholeheartedly of the debate and the vote, though he was terrified by the way in which the Colston statue had been brought down. Black lives *do* matter, but it didn't follow that statues *must* fall, was Mark's view: there were other ways of reckoning with history than denunciation and destruction.

In short, the Burkean in Mark thought that a distinction ought to be made between moral indignation and mob hate – essentially, one between the American and the French Revolutions. In short, Mark had a horror of violence – all forms of it, intellectual and physical. Law, not violence, was there to judge crimes. Conscience, not violence, was there to process guilt.

So he was, as a matter of fact, relieved that Rhodes had not been knocked down, dragged away, and disposed of to the cheering of a crowd as Colston had been. Painfully aware was he of the shockingly short distance, now and again in history, between pulling a statue to the ground and pulling an actual man to the ground.

But Mark liked Eilidh and Lorenzo too much to trouble them with his more reserved sentiments. Affirming 'I'm pleased with the vote', he smiled, and turned admiringly to the sweet-scented roses: 'Such a gorgeous wee garden!'

4

By what strange coincidence am I now in the vicinity of Rosanna's father, reflected Mark to himself, as he settled in Lorenzo's apartment off boulevard Raspail.

By what mysterious force, Mark questioned himself, have I come to visit him unannounced, while two months ago the very idea would have left me disconcerted?

Rue Notre-Dame-des-Champs alone now stood between them. Rosanna's father had written from a small street perpendicular to it and not far from the south edge of the Jardin du Luxembourg.

All being well, Mark thought, I will see him fourteen days from now, if he answers the door.

5

Came the last day of July. It was inordinately hot.

Mark stood in front of a three-storeyed house. After a moment of deliberation, he put on a mask, and rang the bell.

An elderly lady came to the door.

'Good morning Madam,' said Mark, 'I'd like to see Mr. Shu – Mr. Shu De An. I'm his son-in-law.'

The old lady was stupefied. 'Mark?' hesitatingly she asked.

'Yes', replied Mark in wonderment.

'Please come in,' she said with delicate affability, and turned as she called to an elderly man appearing behind her: 'Edmund, it's Mark.'

6

After Mark sat down with the couple in their tasteful, book-filled salon, he understood that Edmund was Rosanna's uncle.

'We invited my brother to come and visit us in 2009. Then we made him stay.'

'How so?'

'I'd say by persuasion, but it was more like Fate... He will tell you.'

'Is he here with you – now?'

'Yes, he's upstairs. I'll tell him you are here.' Edmund rose, and with a smile told Mark, 'You can remove your mask; it's perfectly fine with us if you are not at risk. As for us, we have been cautious.'

'Thank you, sir. I quarantined for two weeks after arrival, and shouldn't be putting you at risk.'

'That's most considerate, Mark. Please have a chat with Agnès. I'll be back in a minute.'

7

Speaking impeccable English like Edmund but with a strong French accent, Agnès asked if Mark would like some tea or coffee. Mark said tea would be lovely. He soon learned that Agnès was born in London to Chinese parents, who settled in Paris when Agnès was two.

'They were the same age as Edmund's parents,' said Agnès.

'Did they move to England after the war?'

'During it, actually. They'd both studied in Paris in the thirties, returning to Shanghai before the war broke out full-scale. After four years living in the French concession, when the Japanese occupied the International Settlement, they ran. A year on the run and they ended up in London, thinking they'd go back when things got better. But things never did get better.'

'I understand. They fled the Sino-Japanese War to England, not knowing when they could return. A few years later, your husband's parents fled the civil war to Taiwan, not knowing when they could return.'

'That's right. When Edmund and I first met in the States, within an hour we realised how much our parents had in common.'

'The same generation of cultural élites tossed around by tumultuous events...'

'Yes... I hope this smoky Earl Grey is to your liking. Do you take milk or sugar?'

'Both, thank you. The tea smells divine.'

8

Ten, perhaps fifteen, minutes waiting for Edmund seemed an eternity. Mark was experiencing an unknown feeling of both disorientation and homecoming.

On the shelves he could see books on art and literature in three languages. Suddenly, he was seized by an ineffable desire that Rosanna be there by his side. She would be emotional, no doubt, and he would calmly hold her hand. All her life, Rosanna had not known that her uncle and aunt lived in Paris. All those years, she had not imagined one day seeing her father again.

Mark felt a bittersweet melancholy engulfing his heart when he heard Edmund descend the stairs.

'Mark, do come with me. He's waiting for you in his study.'

'How is he?'

'Overwhelmed. He'd been worried about you since the pandemic began.'

Mark followed him. A quarter of an hour, he thought to himself, since I met Agnès and Edmund, and yet I feel they are my family – how can this be?

9

There he stood, a thin and frail figure at the door, a cane in his hand, greeting Mark with an almost undetectable smile.

Mark was taken aback when he saw Rosanna's father looking vastly older than his brother Edmund.

'I only read your letter this month; I'd been away this semester.' Mark courteously explained after being seated. It was a cosy little study. A desk stood by the window. Books covered both walls, against one of which was a comfortable Morris chair, in which Mark now sank.

'It's marvellous that you are here.' Shu De An spoke softly from his wicker chair. His voice was weak, and his intonation distinct.

'It was very thoughtful of you to write. We were indeed rather imprudent earlier on.'

'Everyone was. It's normal. It's human nature.' Shu De An sounded detached and powerless as if evoking ancient history.

Mark did not feel much like talking about the pandemic either. By his questions alone was he driven. 'Your brother told me that you were persuaded to stay, ten years ago.'

Old Shu did not respond at once. Looking out the window as though from someone else's room, after a pause he said: 'Edmund found me in Beijing in the spring of 2009. To tell me that our parents had died. For sixty years, I'd made no attempt to contact them.

In the eighties they tried to find me, but failed – I had changed my name in the fifties.'

'So they assumed you were…'

'Dead, yes.'

'But your brother found you eventually.'

'He did. And told me that the last word our mother pronounced, when dying, was my name.'

10

In his mind, Mark saw Rosanna on her deathbed. She had strength enough to look at Luke with a faint smile.

Rosanna would have turned forty-one this August.

For a long minute, neither Mark nor his father-in-law said a word.

A fainthearted comprehension made itself felt. Then, quietly, Shu De An said: 'I am sorry about your loss.'

Mark did not say a word.

Shu De An said: 'I am responsible for this.'

'No, I wouldn't…' Mark shook his head, his gaze fixed to the ground. He did not want this conversation.

'I was never the father I ought to have been. You want to know why I stayed. When Edmund came to Beijing, he was determined to share with me the family fortune left by our parents. I did not want it. I did not need it. My life was in Beijing. He returned two months later, insisting that I visit him and his family. I came with him that autumn. And spent two months with him, Agnès, and their grandchildren. When it was time to leave, I had my suitcase packed, and Pascal and Julie, then eight and nine, held on to me at the door, and cried their eyes out. They asked me not to go. On their tear-stained faces I saw little Rosanna. Rosanna cried and cried the night she and her mother left. But little Rosanna cried in silence. The memory of tears rushing down her innocent face pierced my heart. I broke down. I told the children I would stay.'

11

Mark looked up with misty eyes. He saw a man baring his pierced heart.

'You made the right decision,' said Mark.

'It was my redemption.'

Mark understood the overtone of this choice of word. He pondered for a moment, then said: 'You were able to help bring up the children, in a way.'

'In a way. After their parents divorced, they were

mostly brought up by Agnès and Edmund. I taught them Chinese.'

'They can read, write, and speak Chinese?'

'All of the above.'

'That's terrific!' Mark was impressed. He recalled Rosanna's command of classical Chinese, but refrained from referring to it.

Instead he asked: 'If I may – in 1989, why didn't you leave with Rosanna and her mother?'

A long silence reigned. Then slowly Shu De An said, as if marching on an icy terrain: 'I thought I could not leave my country. I thought I would be a betrayer if I did. I thought my critique and my quest would lose credibility if I chose an easy way out. And that would be a negation of everything in which I believed. The larger part of Tiananmen dissidents who subsequently went abroad – their self-serving performance was what I did not want.'

'I identify with that, and I admire your principles,' said Mark. 'But if you would allow me, leaving your country does not equate with being a dissident activist, and if one were to take into consideration your wife and child…'

'I agree. With thirty years' distance, I see that my perception at the time was coloured, still, by political struggles. And if we were to go further: when Rosanna was born, forty years ago, though I was already middle-aged, it was too early. In hindsight, I had not recovered from... what I had yet to recover from. And when, at an old age, living with my brother and his family, I was at last ready for fatherhood – in short, for my responsibilities as a man – it was too late.'

He stopped, deep in his thoughts. Then, with sadness he looked at Mark: 'To answer your question: in 1989, in favour of my ideas of political duty, I failed my real duty. I let my wife down. And I let my child down.'

After this categorical recapitulation, he added: 'You are speaking to a different person from the one Rosanna and her mother had known, Mark. A person who failed everything, but only now admits it. When I see you – how nice it is to see you – all I can think of is: too late.'

12

Alright. First, one was too young to understand anything. When one understands something, it is too late. That's all rubbish, thought Mark, rubbish.

Without warning, he became angry. He wanted to say to the old man: 'Because you yourself were not ready for parenthood, you decided that your daughter wouldn't be. Because you yourself were damaged by life, you thought life could only damage your child. But you know what? It's never a question of too early or too late. There's only the question of doing the right thing demanded of one in the present.'

Mark gasped for air internally. As much as he had felt at home with Edmund and Agnès downstairs, he felt alienated in Shu De An's presence.

Mark was aware that he was being unfair. Weren't his questions being answered? After all, he had come to question. And yet, almost everything Shu De An said he had in some way expected. Shu De An's remorse was more than appreciated, for want of a better word, but Mark did not feel (or allow himself to feel) sorry for him. To be exact, he knew Shu De An did not want him to feel sorry for him. The sympathy he implicitly had for his father-in-law, he knew it would have embarrassed them both had he shown it.

For now, thought Mark, understanding would suffice. He would press on with his questions. For only in the questioning position might he remain unscathed.

13

Let's pause for a moment, and examine Mark's anger.

Rosanna's father duly answered his son-in-law's questions, baring his pierced heart. It was probably the most he had done for anyone, emotionally speaking. But Mark refused to be moved.

Was this Mark's own defence mechanism kicking in? Was he struggling, still, to forgive?

Understandably, Mark disliked being swayed by emotion. But didn't he come to Paris in order to forgive? – forgiveness being an emotional act, as well as a conscious decision. By crossing over the Channel, he had made the biggest step. Or did he come simply to test the *possibility* of forgiveness?

What Mark did not realise was that, for all he had to mutely lecture his father-in-law on the importance of acting befittingly in the present tense, his own life had long been suspended, fossilised, frozen in a bygone winter that never ended.

14

Mannerly as he was, Mark said to Shu De An: 'I know. Regret is onerous to live with.'

He pressed on with his questions.

'In 1949, why didn't you leave with your parents and brother?'

Old Shu's visage grew weary. It was impossible to tell if he was to say anything, until after a long silence: 'As you may know, Chiang Kai-Shek's government lost popular support during the Second World War. After the war, though we were critical of the Nationalist and the Communist parties in equal measure, my parents were more sceptical, more pessimistic than I. With the Communists winning the civil war, they saw doom; I saw chance. I thought the Communists deserved a chance.'

'You must have been politically very conscious to think so, and headstrong to act according to your thinking, at the age of...'

'Twelve. The war had robbed us of our childhoods. The many wars that ravaged the country ever since the nineteenth century disquieted many a young man and woman. In the same vein, social and political unrest fomented leftist movements in Europe at the time. I was fairly conservative by nature, but was nonetheless sympathetic to some leftist ideals.'

'It's very much of the age, and of the Age.'

'Very much so. Besides, in our context there were more than valid reasons. China, as I saw it, as we all saw it, suffered too many injustices for an entire century. It was insupportable. Whether one party or another would do it temporary harm was for me a secondary consideration. The first imperative was the unification and peace of the country – no foreign invaders; no civil wars – and my relationship to it, to its land and to its people. Come what may, I would not leave it behind.'

'That's very peculiar. I mean, your love for your country that overrode *everything*, even your family, even your own reason. A love, as I see it, that still dominated your whole being in 1989, despite what had happened in between. And yet, it is a love unreciprocated. I wouldn't go so far as to say it's unmerited. But it is so abstract as to be unreal.'

'Real to me. Mark. It was real to me.' Shu De An's voice trembled with severity. 'I was born in March 1937. My parents taught in Nanking, the capital at the time. My maternal grandparents moved there to care for me when my parents, who were archaeologists, travelled. You know the Japanese army massacred the civilians of Nanking in December 1937.'

'I do.'

'In December, my parents were away. The Nationalist government abandoned the capital. Acting on instinct, my grandparents entrusted me to a young colleague of my parents', who took a late train out of the city with me in his arms. All exits were blocked the next day.'

'You survived...'

'I survived. Thanks to my grandparents' instinct. Thanks to the kind young man. I was reunited with my parents weeks later.'

'And... your grandparents?'

'Killed. By the Japanese.'

15

The historian looked with fellow feeling at the man who, since childhood, associated his country's plight with his birth. Could this have led to an exaggerated sense of responsibility, as compensation for the impotence felt vis-à-vis his grandparents' death? Against that life-defining grief, might it have been logical that a young man should identify his country's destiny with his own?

If that be so, Mark could not agree with the logic. But he understood how it might have felt.

With great sincerity he said: 'I am so, so sorry.'

Shu De An withdrew once more into his tired, nearly paralysed countenance.

'Rosanna did not know any of this,' whispered Mark.

'No,' whispered Shu De An.

'Neither did Rosanna's mother.'

'Neither did Rosanna's mother.'

16

Mark did not ask 'Why?', as he sensed the answer to be slumbering in the tempestuous years that we called post-war.

Neither did he wish to tread on painful memories, all the while knowing that, sometimes, the way to understanding was through pain.

With reluctance, he brought up the archive.

'When I read the files of the so-called rightists in the late fifties and early sixties, I thought of you. I imagined your affliction – we are talking about years, decades of it. And I thought I could maybe comprehend.'

This confession failed to bring Shu De An back from

his abstraction.

'I'm sorry,' said Mark, 'you probably don't want to talk about this.'

Looking placid, Shu De An responded in a hushed timbre: 'I never talked about it, for I couldn't bear remembering it. When the pain is too much, the brain has a way of shutting down, putting the pain in a drawer, and not touching it until much later. It's not that one forgets. It's that one has to heal. I needed to heal. Like millions of others, I was in pieces. The country was on its knees.'

'I know, but that is the case no more. Decades – half a century – have passed. The country is no longer on its knees.'

The sun had moved to shine on Mark's face. Summer heat was making itself felt more and more in the room. Shu De An leaned over, and closed the shutters of the window.

He asked if Mark would like some tea or water. Mark said he was fine: 'How about you? Would you like me to fetch some water for you?'

'I'm alright too, thank you.'

17

The hue of the study cooled, as had the temperature. Shu De An's feeble voice carried a distinctive colour of isolation.

'A few years ago, the drawer was finally open, all by itself,' he continued after a long pause. 'In the midst of that wretched period, I never felt I had the right to think about things in my personal context.'

'Except that what had happened could not have been more personal,' Mark said in a small voice.

Shu De An lowered his head. 'The colleague of my parents', the one who took me out of Nanking in his arms...'

'Yes.'

'He died during the Cultural Revolution.'

In that unadorned sentence, Mark heard great sorrow. 'Were you close to him?'

'Very. I went to live with him in Beijing before my parents left. His son was two years old at the time; his daughter only one. But he and his wife took me in, with open arms.'

'They adopted you.'

'Quite literally. I changed my name when I was eighteen, to be his son.'

'I see...'

'A professor of Literature, he taught me everything. The early fifties were the happiest years of my life. Then the Anti-Rightist Campaign began. We were both labelled, but refused to say a bad word about each other.'

'I understand. Everyone was under pressure...'

'I was young; it didn't destroy me. But when the Cultural Revolution came, it was a different matter. We were both betrayed – by his son.'

'Ah!' Mark gasped.

'His son, now twenty years old, told that I was not his brother; that my real parents and brother were in Taiwan. Because of this I was briefly imprisoned. My mentor, an extraordinarily honest man, had been under relentless interrogation, and committed suicide before I was released. His grief-stricken wife went mad. Their son, months later, was killed in an accident.'

Mark exclaimed in disbelief.

A tear came down Shu De An's cheek; he wiped it away. 'So you see, I thought always of him. Of them. I thought much less of myself. After being released, I was sent back to a village in the far north where I'd laboured as a "rightist". For years, all I could think of was them. Year after year, it was minus thirty degrees outside, and I shivered, night after night, reciting the poems we had read together... So many had died. So many suffered more than I. I had, and I have, no right to think about myself.'

'Is that why you never talked about this with anyone, not even with Rosanna's mother?'

'My wife...', Shu De An murmured, looking vacantly down, '... had a simple conception of the world, and a fine capacity to empathise. She felt my pain – that was enough for her to love. Details were of lesser importance to her. And I was grateful for it.'

18

'I think I understand...', said Mark. 'If you would pardon me – did you ever see your wife again?'

Shu De An looked up, his face becoming tender. 'Some years ago, she had an exhibition here, and invited me.'

'How was it?'

'I did not go. We spoke on the phone.'

'Why not?'

Seemingly transported to a faraway place, Shu De An replied, as if dreaming: 'Under the most unlikely circumstances, for reasons beyond us, we had a connection as profound as could be had by two people. The life we had, free of the mundane and of the trivial, was almost improbable. And we had a child. But all was lost... yet kept intact in me...'

'So... by not seeing the love of your life who had become a quasi-stranger, you managed to preserve that improbable... call it perfection; call it illusion.'

'Something like that.'

'Did she understand why you didn't want to see her?' (But of course! thought Mark, we are talking about someone who refused to attend her own daughter's wedding.)

'She did.'

'Remarkable. Do you think she really knew you?'

'Not my life... But my soul.'

'I see... Do forgive me for the intrusion, but you, do you really know her?'

'To the extent that one is capable of knowing another,' said Shu De An demurely, 'I think so.' And he added, looking indulgent: 'Still she calls me from time to time. Crisp, crystal-clear monologues that only she can do. Still I understand what she is trying to do in her art.'

Mark sighed. After a minute of contemplation, he

asked in a low voice: 'And your life... it is I who now know it the best. Why, may I ask, do I have this honour?'

'I owe it to you, Mark.'

'You owe me nothing.'

'You want to understand. And you are predisposed to understand. I see you, and it grieves me to see you, hurt by the passing of Rosanna till this day... There is little now I can do. Let me do what I can.'

For a long time, Mark said nothing. Then he stood up, and came over to Shu De An. With gentleness, he took a pen from the desk behind him, and wrote on a piece of paper:

朝聞道 夕死可矣

Five

1

In response to his father-in-law's avowal, Mark had chosen an archaic way of saying, in the latter's language:
'Enlightened with Truth, one may die with no regret.'
It was his way of saying: 'Not too late.'
Saying anything less would have been inadequate.
Uttering one word more would have been too much for his reserved nature.

2

The tender indulgence on Shu De An's face as he spoke of his long-estranged wife had tugged at Mark's heart.
When Mark was eleven, his father had an affair. It did not last long, and did not destroy the marriage. But the mortifying notion of his mother's anguish stayed permanently with Mark.
Those who have known unhappiness as a child may fear recreating the chagrin, putting off becoming parents. Or they may embrace the plausibility of remedy, bringing happiness to their own offspring.
If Mark was a perfect husband to Rosanna, if he had desired deeply to have children, it was in part a

subconscious correction to all he had perceived to be wrong.

Mark was too kind-hearted to begrudge his father, from whom he yet kept an emotional distance since his eleventh year. Decades passed. A pandemic struck. Mark noted his father's immeasurable protectiveness of his mother, whose severe asthma put her at risk from the virus. Then, and only then, did he allow himself to appreciate his father for the first time.

3

Mark could see, on Shu De An's face, that he had never ceased loving Rosanna's eccentric mother.

He presumed that Rosanna's mother knew.

The truth of a relationship, oftentimes, is unknown but to the two beings concerned.

Mark caught a glimpse of that truth, decades after the marriage of his parents-in-law had run its course. Was it too late? On the contrary. Some verities reveal themselves only after the fact.

After fifty years of marriage, Mark's father held dear his wife in a way that was true to his feelings, true to his intentions, true to himself.

If such was the time it took him to be true, thought Mark, so be it.

4

Mark's unexpected citing of Confucius in its written form visibly moved Shu De An. His eyes becoming animate, he took to muttering energetically:

'The just measure of classical language has been lost in modern times. Evil begins with misnaming things: so-called communists are not communists; so-called rightists are not rightists; so-called democracies are not democracies. When the mind fails to discern sloppy appellations, conceptual muddle ensues.'

He paused, and gazed at Mark's handwriting with an expression that exuded happiness.

5

Mark happened to agree with Shu De An's lament. At bottom, there was more than a touch of the early Renaissance in it, one that illumined his own conviction: that Confucian literati and Renaissance thinkers were cultural twins.

Mark felt, then and there, an affinity with Rosanna's father.

Their mental rapprochement did not end there. For old Shu, recent politics operated above all with distrust, cunning, and inculture, while only polities working with trust, virtue, and culture – antique or modern, monarchic or democratic – came close to being liberal; liberal in the classical sense of the word.

From this perspective, Shu De An maintained that China had long been liberal, long before a borrowed form of republicanism was tried in 1912 (which ended a millennia-old polity to fend off foreign menace) but failed, dividing the country and leaving it to further foreign aggression.

This constitutional revolution, modelled on the French one, created in the ancient land, along with the Sino-Japanese War, what Shu De An called an existential void from which later profited Mao's party – a populist party that knew not how to govern except copying the Soviet Union, and which only began to learn after thirty years of man-made calamity.

With calamity taken as a starting point, the ills of the past century – everywhere they struck – were in Shu De An's view less to do with notional differences of political systems and more a reaction (and overreaction) to unresolved disorders. And the disorders in turn provoked, he averred, by way of ideological strife, stayed rife.

'What is modernity, I sometimes wonder, but continued experimentation with mistakes?' asked Shu De An. 'And what sustains any scheme', he added, 'but continued ability to learn?'

6

With acumen Mark listened. He found Shu De An's sudden energy riveting, and his political position undefinable at best.

'Presumably, this – how should I put it – this pre-modern reading of post-modern politics is the fruit of continued rumination?'

Shu De An sighed, now with less verve in his voice: 'In my youth, I felt as though, in parts of Asia, the Second World War had not concluded, so raw was the emotional pain. In old age, I feel as though, in parts of the West, the Cold War is ongoing, so erect still is the psychic Wall.'

'Which necessarily poses a question to the individual,

in a situation necessarily collective,' commented Mark impromptu, 'namely, how does one live with grief unuttered, and between walls unfallen?'

'That's where the problem began,' admitted Shu De An. 'Especially in contexts less than fortunate, one could easily overreact, as could entire nations, and things could fast become over-politicised without one realising, beyond one's control. It was what I lived through and witnessed, far and near, for the most part of my life. Men dreamt of freedom but built prisons. One built one's own prison...'

'You stayed in your own prison in 1989...', inserted Mark.

'I did. You have understood me... But imagine my astonishment when, thirty years later, on this side of the globe, I see analogous freedom-claiming, prison-building collectives...'

'You do too?'

'It is not my place to make more than a mere observation here. I am a guest here. To return to your question about the individual: with grief unuttered and between walls unfallen, in the last years of my life I have exercised the only political freedom left to be exercised, and that is to be apolitical.'

'Please explain...'

'I try... not to be manipulated by self-absorbed discontent, nor to be moved by elevated rhetoric. Not to resent those blamed, justly or unjustly, for one's own mischance or misdeed, nor to fancy ameliorating the world at one stroke...'

7

This, thought Mark, is getting positively Voltairian; or could it be the counterpoise of a sadder and wiser Confucian, one cloaked with a Taoist, hermitical vestment?

Mark could not quite put his finger on Shu De An's retired but robust stand, until he considered it an idiosyncratic quest for moral measure.

Moral measure as the idea he had first formulated when speaking with Giacomo about the difficulty, and necessity, of suspending judgement – judgement of one's forebears, of immediate history, and of current affairs.

For well over a century, modern intellectuals with the best of intentions felt obligated to take responsibility in one way or another, often failing that responsibility. Often, it would have been an achievement already to comprehend what was going on in this world – before advocating for one doctrine or another; before taking action for one cause or another.

In other words, preparing oneself for political responsibility was more critical than taking it. Suspending judgement until it was fair and ripe. Suspending action until it was guided by sage judgement.

8

One thing had struck Mark: Shu De An's lack of rancour over the persecution he had suffered.

A frame of reference other than that of oppression and victimhood was apparently in force to withstand adversity.

Forbearance, it was called.

The ancients forbore, Mark reflected to himself, while the moderns blame. We have given in to a culture of denouncement, because it is easy. One feels better instantly, gratuitously, pronouncing denouncement.

But loving is the opposite of denouncing, thought Mark. Once, populism seized power in a poet's land; he stayed. Forty years later, his country's future was again uncertain; he stayed.

Another twenty years, and Edmund found his brother in Beijing. Disunited by post-war politics for six decades, they stood face to face, having separately reached a point of political dispassion.

By then, old Shu had been eschewing political discussions for some time, although in more than one way he could scantly recognise the country in which he was born.

Edmund, for his part, had long forsaken the island which, as a young man, he had found too narrowly political and intellectually limiting, before waving his parents farewell in 1963 to study at Harvard, never to return.

9

Forms of apoliticism as ways of seeking freedom – indeed, how *else* might one free oneself from History? This, it seemed to Mark, underlay the brothers' decisions.

Even before taking root in France with fellow architect Agnès, Edmund was neither for nor against either Taiwan's reunification or its independence – a position that hardly endeared him to any persuasion.

To him, there were only the Chinese people in the largest sense; the rest was, and would be, ephemeral.

Edmund escaped History by ignoring it.

10

In the summer of 1989, Shu De An's head turned white. Thence followed historical meditation of a personal nature. Shu De An made peace with his country's far from perfect status quo, deeming it the best scenario that could realistically be had, given China's turbulent recent past – a position that hardly endeared him to any persuasion.

To old Shu, communism was not the real problem, and democracy not the actual issue. Human folly and ambition alternately produced societal failings and success. The West which shook his country out of its tried and tested way of being with guns and cannons was in his view myopic neighbours at the best of times, and his own idealistic countrymen from 1889 to 1989 would have fared better, he reckoned, to resist their neighbours' narcissistic assertions: it had been forgotten that, before Democracy became a slogan, to European thinkers imperial China was the model of political enlightenment. And it oughtn't to be forgotten, suggested Shu De An, that modern democracies as we knew them were themselves products of geohistory, country-specific and going back between decades and centuries: continued assays, not a given.

'For each system has been developed in the course of time,' Shu De An concluded. 'As no two trees in nature are identical, each society is different by necessity. Britain's invasion of us in the nineteenth century opened a century and a half's disorder – monarchic, democratic, anarchic, autocratic, getting worse each time. If ancient despotism has been revived to stabilise my country in the centralised way it had known for two millennia, so be it. By far it is, in this ancient land in modern times, the least damaging form of governing tried.'

No believer of any one system, and wary of his own idealism, Shu De An appeared to care simply for each tree's physiognomy to be respected, not least by itself.

Giving Mark a pained smile, he added woefully: 'If catastrophe after catastrophe is the price a nation has had to pay to relearn how to be in a world that's changed in every way, and if a century and a half is the time it has taken to learn – to continue to learn, for there will surely be more failings to come... so be it.'

Shu De An escaped History in a roundabout way, by

accepting a longer version of it.

11

As Mark well imagined, with surprise and solace the brothers discovered their kindred: an alert lassitude keeping at bay hyped-up aspects of partisan politics.

Confronted with their laissez-faire attitudes, which he knew could not have been easy to acquire or to retain, Mark was free of judgement as to their individual choices: living as we do with difficult histories, we differently wage wars and seek peace.

Mark thought that if more of his countrymen could take a non-partisan step back, England might see fewer disputing kith and kin over its divorce from the Continent.

12

Since the 2016 referendum, Mark's own frustration had turned into resignation.

Like many who had voted to remain, he was appalled at first. 'Big lies and small morals', he said. 'Shortsighted and mean-spirited', he said. With exasperation, he engaged in discussions. It scarcely went well. The opposite side, like him, was emotional.

In the two years that followed, in silence Mark pre-emptively sulked, avoiding all conversations on the subject.

Be that as it may, over the last year he had been calm enough to patiently listen to any argument, and to peacefully share his own thoughts.

For however unthinkable it might have been, he did come to understand where some were coming from.

13

Mark calmed down over Brexit, as he took a longer view of England's history and its relation to Europe, and as he absorbed the fact that, in the wake of the latest recession, many had been disadvantaged by the austerity policies – they needed a culprit for their disgruntlement.

The European Union was made out to be that culprit. Some bought it. Only it was not culpable; neither were the migrant workers, nor the refugees, nor even those who made the policies.

The truth of the matter was: a culprit could not be easily pinpointed.

Disgruntlement stayed unbudging. It demanded to be addressed.

Addressed it was, in the messy fashion emotional addressing was usually.

And now, we had to bite the bullet.

14

'It is wonderful that you and your brother see eye to eye', said Mark to Shu De An, 'in spite of all things external that could have dictated otherwise.'

'Life's mystery and grace', nodded Shu De An, his voice permeated once more by tinges of desolation. 'At the end of the day, Edmund and Agnès taught me what truly mattered: family... and education of the young, which is the one contribution we can make.'

'I quite agree,' said Mark.

15

Agreement faded into silence.

Shu De An thought about Rosanna. Mark thought about Luke. Neither said a word.

Flowers could be late to blossom. Parents could take decades to become. Nature could take all away, in an instant, before one's time.

16

For several months after his return to Oxford, Mark thought of Rosanna's father.

A second lockdown saw him buried in work.

It was a winter like no other for Europeans, separated from one another. It was a winter like any other for Mark, in his perpetual solitude.

Some say this pandemic was the first real world war: a war against a collective crisis; but that may be where the analogy ends.

It was the first dramatic event to have affected the life of virtually everyone on earth.

That experience was at once the same, because shared, and different, depending on where one was.

And the virus wandered, on and on, revealing the true colours of each state, each mortal.

From time to time, Mark would ask a colleague: 'What do you know about the Second Sino-Japanese War?'

In most instances, the answer was a bland look.

To the related question, 'And the fact that China fought as one of the Allies in both world wars, but was badly treated after?', the response was, for the most part, likewise.

History escaped us, thought Mark.

17

A contemporary civil war à l'anglaise, Brexit had tangibly shaken Mark and his peers.

Mark's own argument had been for the future of the young.

Universities had had their share of disservice done to them by austerity, of which the situation that Mark had felt too embarrassed to elaborate to Giacomo was part and parcel. Leaving Europe would mean, in the long run, still less support, still less exchange.

Typical of those whose own youth had thrived in

the hopeful era immediately after the Cold War, Mark trusted that being in Europe – and being 'in the world' – was the auspicious condition under which younger generations would prosper.

When, days after Christmas, he saw on television the Capitol riot in Washington – with disbelief he was glued to the screen, his gesture not unlike how it had been as his teenage self watched nocturnal images of crowds tearing down the Berlin Wall – he realised that the hopeful era he and his generation had known was well and truly over. Whichever 'war' that had been won, thirty years ago, had been lost.

18

Hearing Mark's disheartenment when they spoke on the phone, Giacomo asked if he had ever considered leaving the university, or post-Brexit England.

Mark said he had indeed; but that the answer was no.

He still guarded the credence that education could foster cosmopolitan citizens despite insular conditions – cosmopolitanism being, before all else, a state of mind.

And so, for as long as he worked in education, Mark

needed to believe that all was not lost. For as long as he could provide his students with guidance, his own duty as a citizen, he felt, would not have been unserved.

'Supposing everything had been fine at the university and in the country,' he explained, 'leaving would not have been inconceivable. But all is not well, and I feel compelled to stay.'

'That's counterintuitive,' said Giacomo, 'but also why, I think, you understand the early choices of your father-in-law...'

'I think so.'

Fraternity in his heart, with warmth of feeling Giacomo said: 'You have reconciled with him, Mark. You have forgiven.'

'I do not know, sir, if that's what it is. Granted, for any reconciliation to take place, there must be understanding – understanding is what it is...'

'And what do you understand?'

'That which is not for me to condemn. That which is not for me to forgive.'